Written and illustrated by Teddy Moreta
Copyright © Teddy Moreta 2020
All rights reserved. Published by Camajamo Publishing
Printed in the United States of America

ISBN: 978-1-7332767-2-6
Product Number 050219RK
Version 1.0

Rock and Kite

Written and Illustrated by Teddy Moreta

Rock was a stone who lived in a valley all by himself.

Rock was in search of other stones and felt alone without a purpose.

One day he met Kite, who was looking for a high place to jump from, so she could fly and see all of the valley below.

As Rock and Kite shared their feelings, they quickly became friends.

They decided to walk through the valley together to find more stones and a high place for Kite to launch.

As they reached a stream, Rock stopped and became sad.

"What's wrong," said Kite.

"Stones don't float," replied Rock, "and if I try to cross the stream, I will sink."

"Well, we're lucky we're different," said Kite, "I can float on water for a little while. You can climb on my back, and we can float across together."

So Rock climbed onto Kite, and they both safely crossed the stream.

The two friends continued on and searched the valley for several days and nights.

Eventually, they came across a mountain, piled high with stones of every shape and size.

"YESSSSS!" said Rock as he smiled, "Now I have so many other friends like me to be with, I am soooooooo happy."

"WOWEEEEE!" said Kite, "I will be able to see the whole valley from the top of this mountain. Now I have a high place to jump from and fly."

The two friends then climbed to the top of the mountain together.

Rock found a place toward the top where he would fit perfectly among all his new friends.

Kite saw a great spot to jump from to fly over the valley below.

Suddenly, Kite's joy changed to panic. "UGGGGHHHHH," she cried out as she looked down, "There are thorn bushes up here, and my tail will get tangled in them if I jump."

Rock winked and said with a smile, "We're lucky we're different, thorn bushes don't bother me. You can climb on my back and jump over them."

Kite then climbed on top of Rock and waited for the right moment. The wind blew with a big "WHEWWWWWW!" and Kite smiled and jumped off the mountain.

Just as Kite began to fly, Rock jumped on her back, thinking they could fly together, but they both began to fall quickly to the valley floor.

"WHOOOOOOOHHH!" said Kite, "If you stay on my back we will both crash."

19

Rock then remembered that they are both different, with unique gifts that are not the same.

So he quickly jumped off and stood with the other stones on the mountain so his friend could fly.

21

And every day after that, Kite climbed to the top of the mountain and jumped off her friend Rock to fly over the valley.

And every time, she would look back and see Rock surrounded by his friends, fitting in perfectly, and she'd smile, knowing he had found his purpose.

"Just Be You!"